P9-DVP-243

Busy School

**Created by Susan Baum
of the Gear Design Team ™**

Grosset & Dunlap • New York

Copyright © 1988 by GEAR Inc. All rights reserved.
Published by Grosset & Dunlap, Inc., a member of The Putnam Publishing Group, New York.
GEAR BEAR is a trademark of GEAR Inc. Printed in Singapore.
Published simultaneously in Canada.
Library of Congress Catalog Card Number: 87-83327   ISBN 0-448-09279-4
A B C D E F G H I J

clock

classroom

wastebasket

alphabet

bell

Aa Bb Cc

It's nine o'clock. The school bell rings. All the busy school bears hang up their coats, find their seats, and wave hello to their friends.

"Come on in. Don't be shy," says Gear Bear to Puppy Love, who has come to visit the class.

Dd Ee Ff Gg Hh Ii Jj Kk Ll

hook

hanger

coat

lunch box

gym bag

desk and chair

flag

picture

window

teacher

"I pledge allegiance to the flag," say the school bears with Teacher Bear as they place their hands over their hearts. They promise to be good bears, to work hard, and to have fun, too! When Puppy Love hears that, he's ready to join in.

students

First, it's time for show-and-tell.
Gear Bear brings Puppy Love to
the front of the classroom.
"This is my best friend and loyal
buddy," he says pointing to Puppy
Love. Puppy Love's ears tingle
because he feels proud.

puppet

table

football

souvenir

cap

truck

seashells

•FLORIDA•

BEARS

There's so much to see and do
in the science room.

dinosaur models

space map

rocket

fish tank

USA

magnet   globe

microscope

Some of the school bears gather around the table to hear the Professor talk about dinosaurs. Gear Bear feeds the hungry fish while a classmate looks at the globe.

The school bears take time out from work to eat lunch and play. The warm sunshine feels good as they run in the playground. Puppy Love is really enjoying school now!

see-saw

hopscotch

1 2 3 5 6 7 8 9 10

swings

slide

picnic table

bench

Back in the library, the school bears settle down
to hear a story. They lie quietly on their mats
and listen to the gentle sound of Teacher Bear's
voice. Puppy Love's eyes begin to close...

mat

READ BOOKS

poster

bookcase

map

plant

storybook

books

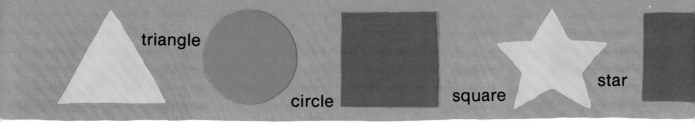

triangle
circle
square
star

"Uh, oh. I need help!" cries Gear Bear. He is having trouble figuring out his math problem. Puppy Love tries to help him on the computer. One classmate already knows the answer and raises his hand to get the teacher's attention.

eraser
paper
pencil

rectangle

SEPTEMBER

		1	2	3	4	5
6	7	8	9	10	11	12
13	14	15	16	17	18	19
20	21	22	23	24	25	26
27	28	29	30			

calendar

triangle

$$\begin{array}{r} 2 \\ + 3 \\ \hline ? \end{array}$$

$$\begin{array}{r} 2 \\ + 3 \\ \hline 5 \end{array}$$

computer

abacus

In art class the school bears are making special hats. Gear Bear also makes a heart for Puppy Love to wear.

paper

paint bottles

cabinets

ruler

crayons

PASTE

paste

"Please pass the paste," says one school bear.
"How do I look?" asks another.

sink

paintbrush

scissors

ribbon

Now everyone is ready to make lots of noise in the rhythm band. *T-t-ting!* goes the triangle. *Bang!* goes the drum. *Toot!* goes the horn. *Chick-a chick-a!* go the maracas. Gear Bear takes the cymbals and makes the loudest noise of all, *CRASH-SH-SH-SH-SH!*

horn

drum

triangle

maraca

musical notes

baton

music stand

cymbals

school bus

The school bears
march right out of the building.
They've worked hard and had
fun, and now the busy school day is over.

"Come, Puppy Love, it's time
to go home!"

See you tomorrow!